MY 1ST
GRAPHIC
NOVEL®

Bus Ride
BULLY

MY FIRST GRAPHIC NOVELS ARE PUBLISHED BY STONE ARCH BOOKS
A CAPSTONE IMPRINT
1710 ROE CREST DRIVE
NORTH MANKATO, MINNESOTA 56003
WWW.CAPSTONEPUB.COM

COPYRIGHT © 2011 BY STONE ARCH BOOKS

Library of Congress Cataloging-in-Publication data is available on the
Library of Congress website.

ISBN-13: 978-1-4342-2059-2 (library binding)
ISBN-13: 978-1-4342-3101-7 (paperback)

Summary: Gavin hates riding the bus because of Max, the bus bully.
When Max is gone for a few days, Gavin gets worried. Find out what
happens between Gavin and the bus bully.

Art Director: BOB LENTZ
Graphic Designer: EMILY HARRIS
Production Specialist: MICHELLE BIEDSCHEID

Bus Ride BULLY

by Cari Meister

illustrated by Rémy Simard

STONE ARCH BOOKS
a capstone imprint

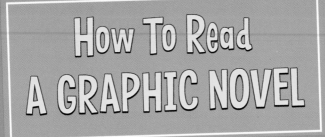

How To Read
A GRAPHIC NOVEL

Graphic novels are easy to read. Boxes called panels show you how to follow the story. Look at the panels from left to right and top to bottom.

Read the word boxes and word balloons from left to right as well. Don't forget the sound and action words in the pictures.

The pictures and the words work together to tell the whole story.

Gavin did not like to ride the bus. He did not like the way it looked.

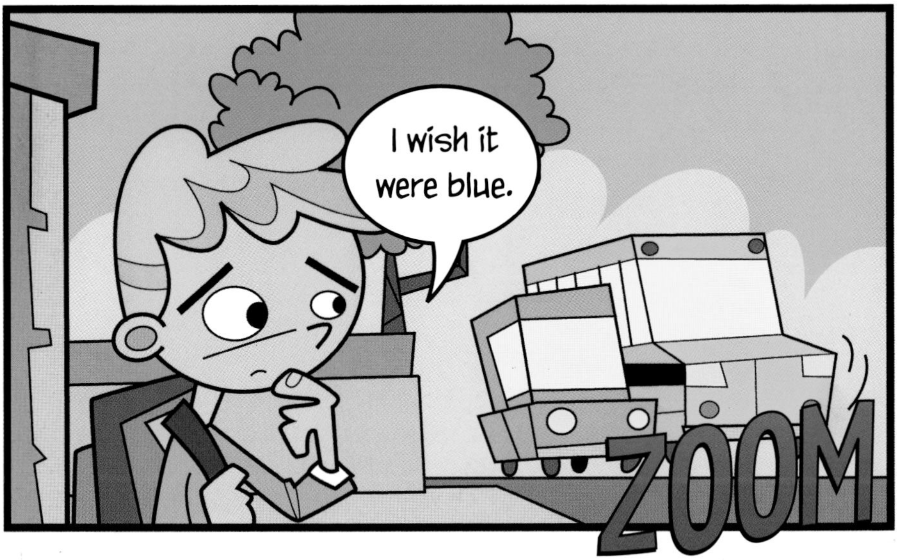
I wish it were blue.
ZOOM

He did not like the way it smelled.

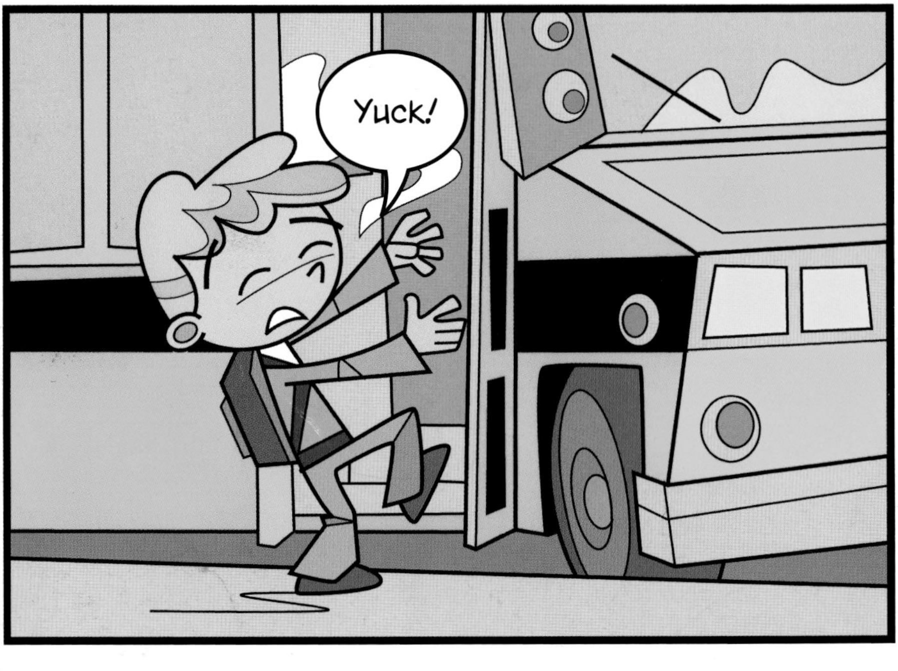
Yuck!

Most of all, he did not like Max.

Max was big. Max was smelly. Max was a bully.

Every day, Max tripped Gavin.

Every day, Max teased Gavin.

The bus driver didn't notice. He was too busy looking at his watch.

He was too busy telling the loud kids to be quiet.

Max was not loud, so the bus driver left him alone.

Gavin tried to hide from Max.

But Max always found him. Max made
Gavin share his seat.

He made Gavin share his snack, too.

Gavin couldn't wait to get off the bus.

One day, Max was gone. Gavin was happy.

He could eat his snack in peace.

He could look out the window in peace.

Max was gone the next day, too. Then Gavin found out why. Max had a bike accident.

Max was okay, but he had to stay home for a few days.

Gavin got off the bus.

As he walked home, he thought about Max.

Max didn't seem to have any friends.

The next day after school, Gavin went to
Max's house.

Max's mom came to the door. She was happy
to see Gavin.

Max was up in his room. Gavin was a little scared to go in.

Max was in bed. He did not look mean in his pajamas.

Max shared his animal cookies with Gavin.

Max showed Gavin his dinosaur collection. He gave Gavin a T. rex to take home.

Gavin couldn't believe it. Max was being nice!

Soon, Max was back on the bus.

Gavin didn't try to hide anymore.

Max, over here!

Gavin didn't mind riding the bus anymore.
He even started to like it.

The End

About the AUTHOR

Cari Meister is the author of many books for children, including the My Pony Jack series and *Luther's Halloween*. She lives on a small farm in Minnesota with her husband, four sons, three horses, one dog, and one cat. Cari enjoys running, snowshoeing, horseback riding, and yoga.

ABOUT THE ILLUSTRATOR

Rémy Simard began his career as an illustrator in 1980. Today he creates computer-generated illustrations for a large variety of clients. He has also written and illustrated more than 30 children's books in both French and English, including *Monsieur Noir et Blanc*, a finalist for Canada's Governor's Prize. To relax, Rémy likes to race around on his motorcycle. Rémy resides in Montreal with his two sons and a cat named Billy.

GLOSSARY

ACCIDENT (AK-si-duhnt) — an unplanned event

BULLY (BUL-ee) — a person who picks on other people

COLLECTION (kuh-LEK-shuhn) — a group of things gathered over a period of time

PAJAMAS (puh-JAM-uhz) — a set of clothes to sleep in

TEASED (TEEZD) — said mean things to someone

1. Do you remember the first time you rode on a bus? What was it like?

2. Were you surprised when you found out that Max thinks Gavin is his best friend? Explain your answer.

3. If you were Gavin, would you go see Max at his house? Discuss your answer.

WRITING PROMPTS

1. At the beginning of the story, Max is a bully. Write a small paragraph explaining how you would deal with a bully.

2. The bus driver has a hard time controlling the children. Make a list of three bus rules.

3. At the end of the story, Max and Gavin are friends. Draw a picture of your best friend and write a small paragraph about him or her.

The First Step into
GRAPHIC NOVELS

These books are the perfect introduction
to the world of safe, appealing graphic novels. Each
story uses familiar topics, repeating patterns, and core
vocabulary words appropriate for a beginning reader.
Combine the entertaining story with comic book panels,
exciting action elements, and bright colors and
a safe graphic novel is born.

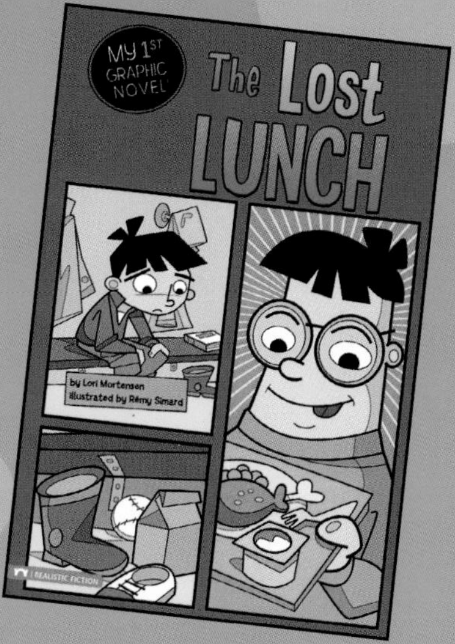
MY 1ST GRAPHIC NOVEL
The Lost LUNCH
by Lori Mortensen
illustrated by Rémy Simard
REALISTIC FICTION

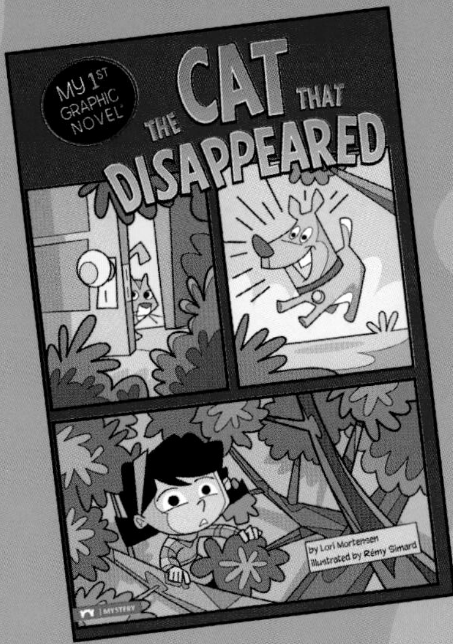
MY 1ST GRAPHIC NOVEL
THE CAT THAT DISAPPEARED
by Lori Mortensen
illustrated by Rémy Simard
MYSTERY

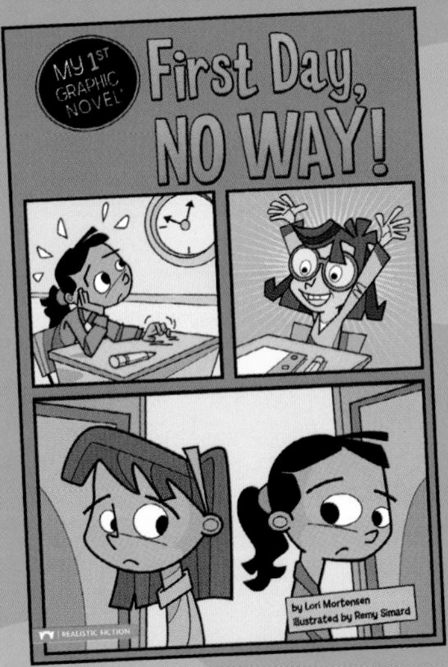
MY 1ST GRAPHIC NOVEL
First Day, NO WAY!
by Lori Mortensen
illustrated by Rémy Simard
REALISTIC FICTION

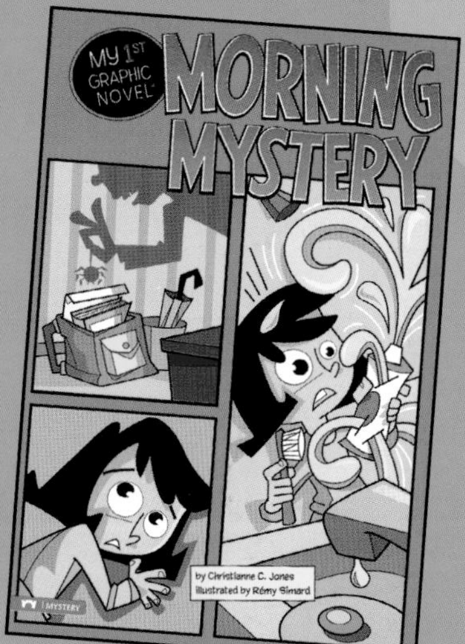
MY 1ST GRAPHIC NOVEL
MORNING MYSTERY
by Christianne C. Jones
illustrated by Rémy Simard
MYSTERY

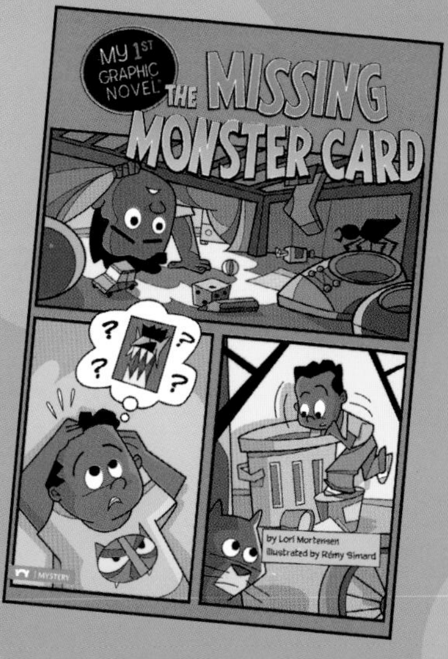
MY 1ST GRAPHIC NOVEL
THE MISSING MONSTER CARD
by Lori Mortensen
illustrated by Rémy Simard
MYSTERY

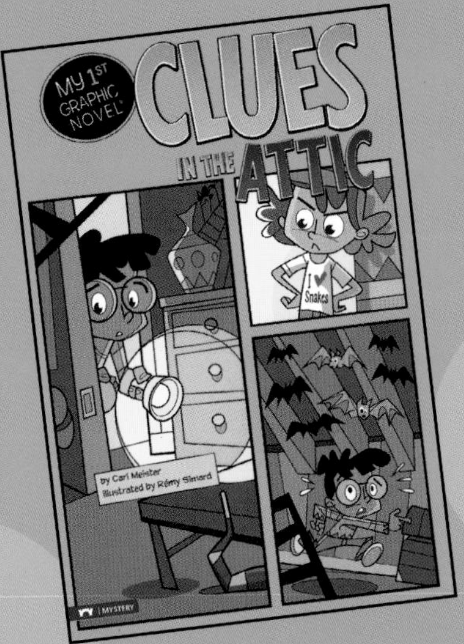
MY 1ST GRAPHIC NOVEL
CLUES IN THE ATTIC
I ♥ Snakes
by Carl Meister
illustrated by Rémy Simard
MYSTERY